THE
3
LITTLE
PIGS

First Meadow Mouse paperback edition 1997
Reissued in paperback in 2004

Groundwood Books / Douglas & McIntyre
720 Bathurst Street, Suite 500, Toronto, Ontario M5S 2R4

Distributed in the USA by Publishers Group West
1700 Fourth Street, Berkeley, CA 94710

We acknowledge for their financial support of our publishing program the Canada Council for the Arts, the Government of Canada through the Book Publishing Industry Development Program (BPIDP), the Ontario Arts Council and the Government of Ontario through the Ontario Media Development Corporation's Ontario Book Initiative.

National Library of Canada Cataloging in Publication
The 3 little pigs / illustrated by Marie-Louise Gay.
"A Groundwood Book."
ISBN 0-88899-211-4 (bound).–ISBN 0-88899-639-X (pbk.)
I. Gay, Marie-Louise II. Title: Three little pigs.
PZ8.1.G25Th 1994 j398.24'529734 C94-930726-2

The illustrations in this book are in pen and ink and watercolor.
Printed and bound in China

A Groundwood Book
Douglas & McIntyre
Toronto Vancouver Berkeley

THERE was an old sow with three little pigs, and as she had not enough to keep them, she sent them out to seek their fortunes.

The first that went off met a man with a bundle of straw and said, "Please, man, give me that straw to build me a house."

Which the man did, and the pig built a house with it.

Presently along came a wolf, who knocked at the door and said, “Little pig, little pig, let me come in.”

To which the pig answered, “No, no, by the hair on my chinny-chin-chin.”

“Then I’ll huff, and I’ll puff, and I’ll blow your house in.”

So the wolf huffed, and he puffed, and he blew the house in, and ate up the little pig.

The second little pig met a man with a bundle of wood and said, "Please, man, give me that wood to build a house."

Which the man did, and the pig built his house.

Then along came the wolf, who said, "Little pig, little pig, let me come in."

"No, no, by the hair on my chinny-chin-chin."

"Then I'll puff, and I'll huff, and I'll blow your house in."

So he huffed, and he puffed, and he puffed, and he huffed, and at last he blew the house in, and ate up the little pig.

The third little pig met a man with a load of bricks and said, "Please, man, give me those bricks to build a house."

So the man gave him the bricks, and the pig built his house with them.

Soon the wolf came and said, "Little pig, little pig, let me come in."

"No, no, by the hair on my chinny-chin-chin."

"Then I'll huff, and I'll puff, and I'll blow your house in."

Well, he huffed, and he puffed, and he huffed, and he puffed, and he puffed and huffed...but he could *not* blow the house in.

When the wolf found that he could not, with all his huffing and puffing, blow the house in, he said, "Little pig, I know where there is a nice field of turnips."

"Where?" said the little pig.

"In Mr. Smith's field, and if you will be ready tomorrow morning I will call for you, and we will go together and get some for dinner."

"Very well," said the little pig. "I will be ready. What time do you mean to come?"

"Oh, at six o'clock."

Well, the little pig got up at five and got the turnips before the wolf came, which he did about six.

"Little pig, are you ready?" the wolf said.

"Ready?" said the little pig. "I have been and come back again and got a nice potful of turnips for dinner."

The wolf felt very angry at this, but thought that he could trick the little pig somehow or other, so he said, "Little pig, I know where there is a nice apple tree."

"Where?" said the pig.

"Down at Merry Garden," replied the wolf. "And if you will not deceive me, I will come for you at five o'clock tomorrow, and we can get some apples."

Well, the little pig bustled up the next morning at four o'clock and went off for the apples, hoping to get back before the wolf came. But he had farther to go this time and had to climb the tree. Just as he was coming down, he saw the wolf which, as you may well suppose, frightened him very much.

When the wolf came up, he said, "Little pig, what? Are you here before me? Are they nice apples?"

"Yes, very," said the little pig. "I will throw you down one."

And he threw it so far, that while the wolf was gone to pick it up, the little pig jumped down and ran home.

The next day the wolf came again and said to the little pig, "Little pig, there is a fair at Shanklin this afternoon. Will you go?"

"Oh, yes," said the pig, "I will go. What time shall you be ready?"

"At three," said the wolf.

So the little pig went off before the time as usual. He got to the fair and bought a butter churn, which he was carrying home when he saw the wolf coming. Then he could not tell what to do. So he climbed into the churn to hide, and by doing so turned it around.

The butter churn rolled down the hill with the pig in it, which frightened the wolf so much he ran home without going to the fair.

Then he went to the little pig's house and told him how frightened he had been by a great round thing that had come down the hill.

"Hah, I frightened you then," said the little pig. "I went to the fair and bought a butter churn, and when I saw you, I got in it and rolled down the hill."

The wolf was very angry indeed and declared he would climb down the chimney and eat up the little pig.

When the little pig saw what the wolf was about, he hung up a pot full of water and made a blazing fire. Just as the wolf was coming down the chimney, the little pig took off the cover, and in fell the wolf. The little pig put on the cover again in an instant, boiled up the wolf, and ate him for supper...

and lived happily ever after.